BED BOUNCERS

by Kimberley Knutson

Macmillan Books for Young Readers • New York

Macmillan Books for Young Readers
An imprint of Simon & Schuster Children's Publishing Division
Simon & Schuster Macmillan
1230 Avenue of the Americas
New York, New York 10020

Printed and bound in Singapore on recycled paper.
First Edition

10 9 8 7 6 5 4 3 2 1

The text of this book is set in 16 pt. ITC Leawood Medium.
The illustrations were done in handmade paper and collage.

Library of Congress Cataloging-in-Publication Data
Knutson, Kimberley.
Bed bouncers / Kimberley Knutson. — 1st ed.
p.   cm.
Summary: A rhyming fantasy of children whose bed bouncing takes
them all the way to the moon and back.
ISBN 0-02-750871-4
[1. Beds—Fiction.   2. Bedtime—Fiction.   3. Stories in rhyme.]
I. Title.
PZ8.3.K7525Be   1995
[E]—dc20   94-14410

To my husband, Michael

We bed bouncers bounce up
when no one's around.
We slip from the sheets
without making a sound.

We peek
out the
door…

then spring up on the bed,
to bounce up
and jounce up
above every head!

We vault and we leap,
we pounce and we pop,
attempting a backward
twist-fish-belly flop.

And while we are bouncing
and springing and sproinging,
sneaking and creaking
and banging and boinging…

we see that our ceiling
is starting to fade.
And soon we soar off
in a floating parade.

We head for the heavens
as far as we dare…

so high we hear only
the silence of air.
Swoosh…whoosh…
shoosh…hush…

deep into the peace
of the velvety night.
Then down again—*flash!*—
like a meteorite.

We meet with a runaway birthday balloon.

We tickle the stars

and we swing on the moon.

We meet other bouncers
from all different lands,

compare and trade pillows,
and shake all their hands.

All ages and sizes
and colors of skin,
we tumble
together
and giggle
and grin.

Beginners and experts,
some fast and some slow,
all bouncing while watching
the cities below.

We try the trick
bed bouncers seldom survive:
The one-handed rotating
cannonball dive! (We do five.)

We cheer and we holler!
We scream and we shout!

And promise to play again
next time we're out.

Then *swoop!*
We all somersault
head over feet…
bounce back to the earth
and land right in our sheets.

We bounce and we jounce
and we muss up the spread...
till someone shouts,

"Don't jump around on the bed!"

We dive for the blankets
and burrow down deep.
Quick! Squeeze our eyes shut
and pretend we're asleep.

We lie very still
(but take one stealthy glance)
and patiently listen
and wait for the chance

to toss off the covers
and fly through the air!
It's risky—and only
real bed bouncers dare.